D0357194

RAKSHA
THE MIRROR
DEMON

With special thanks to Michael Ford

For Joel

www.beastquest.co.uk

ORCHARD BOOKS
338 Euston Road, London NW1 3BH
Orchard Books Australia
Level 17/207 Kent St, Sydney, NSW 2000

A Paperback Original
First published in Great Britain in 2011

Beast Quest is a registered trademark of Beast Quest Limited
Series created by Beast Quest Limited, London

Text © Working Partners Limited 2011
Cover and inside illustrations by Steve Sims © Orchard Books 2011

A CIP catalogue record for this book is available
from the British Library.

ISBN 978 1 40831 323 7

1 3 5 7 9 10 8 6 4 2

Printed and bound by CPI Group (UK) Ltd, Croydon, CR0 4YY

The paper and board used in this paperback are natural recyclable
products made from wood grown in sustainable forests.
The manufacturing processes conform to the environmental
regulations of the country of origin.

Orchard Books is a division of Hachette Children's Books,
an Hachette UK company.

www.hachette.co.uk

RAKSHA
THE MIRROR
DEMON

BY ADAM BLADE

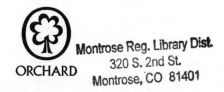

STORY ONE

Hail All!

My name is Kapra. You may already know my daughter – the snivelling wretch, Petra. If you think her magic or any of the spells you've seen in Avantia are impressive, then you're fools! I and my wizard companion, Feldric, are about to visit the kingdom and call the most fearsome Beast ever from the Lake of Light.

Tom likes his Quests, doesn't he? But can this one really be won by the nephew of a blacksmith? Don't make me laugh! I'll enjoy watching Tom brought to his knees. I might even see him die. I live in hope... With the power of seven Beasts, who knows what I can achieve?

Yours in delight and anticipation,

Kapra the Gorgonian Witch

CHAPTER ONE

GUARDIANS OF THE KINGDOM

Up in Aduro's turret chamber, surrounded by scrolls and mysterious chests, Daltec tapped the crystal ball with a fingernail and peered at the surface. The glass remained dull, and grey clouds swirled inside.

"Did Aduro ever show you how this worked?" he asked.

Elenna nudged Tom with her elbow and he tried not to grin. So far, the

Good Wizard Aduro's new boy apprentice wasn't doing very well.

"He just waved his hand over the top," said Tom. "Then the mists would clear and show what was happening around the kingdom."

"Oh, right!" said Daltec. He closed his eyes and swished his hand over the ball.

Nothing happened.

Elenna burst out laughing, which she quickly hid beneath a coughing fit. Daltec looked at Tom helplessly and Tom shrugged back.

I'm not the magician around here, Tom thought. As Daltec tried again, Tom wondered how Taladon was getting on in Gorgonia. His father had left a few days earlier with Aduro and King Hugo on a mission. It must have been serious, because they'd had to cancel the Knights' Banquet.

So far there'd been no word from them. Tom had wanted to go as well – the thought of facing a Quest alongside his father filled him with pride – but Aduro had insisted he and Elenna remain in Avantia. The Kingdom must never be unprotected, he'd said.

"Got it!" Daltec yelled.

Tom snapped his eyes back to the crystal ball, which now showed Tagus proudly galloping across the plains, herding cattle. With another wave of Daltec's hand, the scene shifted to the Western Seas, where Sepron was tugging a ship to shore over stormy waves. Next came Nanook, shovelling great armfuls of snow and ice to clear a road in the Frozen North. Tom's heart swelled with pride.

"All the Beasts are doing their jobs and keeping the kingdom safe," Elenna said.

The door thudded open, and screeches suddenly filled the chamber. Tom jerked around, hand moving to the hilt of his sword. A little girl was being pursued by a young servant boy. Their laughter stopped when they saw Tom and his companions. Daltec quickly wafted his hand over the crystal ball and the glass clouded once again.

"I...I'm... We're sorry," said the boy.

"We were just playing tag," added the girl.

"That's all right," Tom said, smiling. "But you should take your game elsewhere."

The boy and girl rushed out of the room.

"I think we're finished here," said Tom to Elenna. "Let's go and inspect the armoury."

"I'll stay and get some practice with this ball," sighed Daltec.

Tom led the way out of the room and headed down the spiral steps. He could hear the echoing sound of the children playing below near King

Hugo's banqueting hall.

A wail of alarm pierced the air.

"That didn't sound like someone having fun," said Elenna, her eyes wide.

"Let's go!" said Tom. He took the steps two at a time. As they reached the bottom, he saw the children rush from King Hugo's banqueting hall, fear etched into their faces. They cowered against the opposite wall and clung to each other.

Tom drew his sword. "What is it?" he asked.

The boy nodded towards the hall doors, which had almost swung closed.

Elenna deftly drew an arrow from her quiver and set it to the taut bowstring.

"I'll go first," said Tom.

He kicked the doors. They burst wide open and he leapt into the room. At first he couldn't see anything amiss. The central table, which could easily seat fifty people, was bare but for the tall candlesticks along the centre. Crystal chandeliers hung from the ceiling, catching the glinting light from outside. Fine tapestries lined the walls, interspersed with tall, polished mirrors.

"I don't understand," said Elenna, drawing alongside him. "What are they afraid of?"

A movement drew Tom's glance. His reflection in the mirror opposite seemed to wobble. Peering closer, he saw the surface of the glass ripple out from the centre, as if a stone had been dropped into a still pool of water.

"That's not possible..." he muttered, moving closer. Now all the mirrors acted in the same way, the glass distorting and wobbling as he passed. His image stretched and shrank in the ebbing reflections.

As he moved nearer to the glass, he saw a shadow behind him.

"Look out!" Elenna cried.

Tom spun around to see a figure in a black cloak lunging at him.

He ducked under the blur of a staff, then brought the flat of his sword down on the man's wrist. The attacker howled in pain and dropped his weapon. As it clattered on the floor, Tom saw it was a wizard's staff, one end of which was moulded into a heavy bronze club.

If I hadn't ducked, that would have smashed my skull! he thought.

As the black-clad man nursed his bruised wrist, Elenna rushed forward and snatched up the staff. A snarl came from the doorway, where Silver stood at the entrance, hackles raised and eyes narrowed. He padded slowly towards the stranger, who backed away until he bumped into the table. Beneath his cloak he wore a tunic of emerald silk, embroidered with coils of gold thread. Strands of grey hair were plastered across his head, and he peered at them out of pouchy eyes.

"Silver must have heard the commotion," said Elenna.

Tom levelled his sword at his attacker. "Who are you, and where did you come from?"

The man's eyes flickered to the side. Tom followed his gaze to the largest mirror at the end of the room. The glass rippled, then ballooned out. Tom made out five spikes pushing from the inside, stretching the silvery surface. Something, or someone, was trying to push through. He lifted his sword away from the man, and pointed it towards the glass.

A hand broke though the mirror, with nails like filthy talons, but the glass didn't shatter. An arm followed,

then came a whole body, stumbling
into the room. A woman in golden
robes staggered against King Hugo's
carved chair, then righted herself.

Tom knew right away, from the
cruel glitter of her eyes, that a new
enemy had arrived in Avantia.

CHAPTER TWO

THE MIRROR OF RAKSHA

"You fool!" snarled the woman,
pointing at the older man.
"Outsmarted by a boy!"

Tom took a stride towards her.
"Watch who you call a boy," he
warned.

The woman in the golden cloak
snapped her fingers towards Elenna.

"No!" Elenna yelled.

Tom saw her struggling to keep hold

of the staff, tugging against an invisible force. Finally, it was snatched from her grasp and flew into the waiting hand of the man. He quickly jabbed with the brass end, catching Tom in his stomach. Tom fell with a grunt, struggling to gather his breath. Silver pounced with a growl, but the wizard caught him with the staff too, sending the brave wolf sprawling to the foot of one of the mirrors.

"Keep your mutt under control,"
he said, in a squeaky voice.

The woman paced to one of the
windows. With her robes swishing
across the ground, she almost seemed
to glide. The wizard scurried to join
her with his staff, as Elenna came to
Tom's side and put an arm around
his shoulders. "Are you all right?"

"Never mind me," he said. "We
need to stop these two."

"Where's that fool Hugo?" asked
the woman, her eyes scanning the
courtyard below.

"I thought he'd be here," whined
the wizard. "This is usually when
he holds the Knights' Banquet."

"Well, he isn't!" she spat. "And
I can't see anyone gnawing on
a chicken thigh, can you?"

Tom climbed to his feet. "Who

are you?" he asked, "and what do you want?"

The woman turned, anger twisting her mouth. With a jerk of her hand, she sent a bolt of purple light across the chamber. It smashed into the wall beside his head, scorching a hole in the tapestry that hung there. Tom noticed that the light had turned a candle on the table into a molten heap of wax.

With more purple sparks fizzing at her fingertips, the woman walked slowly towards Tom.

"Who are you to question me?" she asked, letting out an odd chuckle.

Now she was closer, Tom could study her face more closely. She had plump, red cheeks, and her slightly greying hair hung in tangled, unwashed strands around her face.

And that laugh, Tom thought.
I recognise you...

"You look like Petra the Witch!" he said.

The woman chuckled. "Well done!" she clapped sarcastically. "My daughter mentioned you were a clever one."

"Your daughter?" said Elenna. She was crouched beside Silver, who was licking the back of her hand.

"My name is Kapra," said the witch, "and that snivelling wretch Petra is my offspring. This" – she cast a hand towards the wizard – "is the supposedly great wizard of Gorgonia, Feldric. Feldric, do you have the mirror?"

The wizard patted his robes several times and slipped a hand into his emerald tunic, his face going pale.

"Er... I must have dropped it when I came through."

Kapra hissed. "Well, find it! That's our only way of locating the Lake of Light."

Tom frowned. *The Lake of Light's just a fairy story!*

Feldric's eyes passed around the room from mirror to mirror. "I can't remember..."

Kapra rolled her eyes and lunged suddenly at Tom, seizing him by the collar. "Then *you* can tell us! Where's the Lake of Light?"

Tom shook his head. He'd heard of the lake in childhood tales, but that's all it was – a story. It was meant to be a great, shimmering lake in a hidden valley.

"I've no idea," he said. "I don't think..."

Kapra threw him aside with more strength than Tom could have imagined in those pudgy arms. He bounced over the table, landing in a heap on the other side.

"Useless!" she bellowed.

Under the table, Tom saw Elenna

whisper in Silver's ear. "Go, boy!"

Tom stood gingerly as the wolf bounded towards Petra's mother. Kapra whipped her golden cloak aside. From her neck hung a green pendant, an engraved stone that she held in front of her face. At once, her grey hair seemed to thicken and grow slimy with scales. The ends swelled into snakes' heads. One by one, the snakes dropped away onto the floor, leaving her head bald with mottled pale skin. The vipers slithered across the ground towards Silver, winding around his legs. The wolf backed away, yowling in panic.

"Silver!" Elenna cried.

Kapra restored the stone to the folds of her cloak, and the snakes retreated, climbing under her robes. Her hair grew once more, covering

her baldness. She let out an evil
chuckle.

"I won't tell you again – keep your
pet in check," she said.

Feldric was making his way from
mirror to mirror, plunging his arm
into each rippling surface.

"Haven't you found it yet?"
muttered Kapra. "If the boy won't
help us find the lake, we still need
the Mirror of Raksha."

Who, or what, is Raksha? Tom
wondered.

As Feldric reached through the
glass of the mirror beside the grand
fireplace, his eyes widened. "Aha!"
he said. "Found it!"

With a tug, he withdrew his arm.
He held an object aloft in triumph.

"Finally!" muttered Kapra.

Feldric gripped the handle of an

ornate silver hand mirror. Jewels
encrusted the rim, and it was carved
into a pattern of writhing snakes.
Tom couldn't help a shudder.

"You shouldn't have that!" Daltec's
voice rang out. Tom saw their friend
standing in the doorway with his
staff. The frightened children must
have run off to find him. The wizard
apprentice stepped into the room.

"It was stolen from Aduro."

"We're only borrowing it," snarled Kapra. "Be gone, young one, and practice your spells."

"With pleasure!" Daltec said. He raised his staff, muttering an incantation under his breath. Kapra laughed and flung out a hand. Purple light sizzled from her fingertips and struck the apprentice in the chest, passing right through him. As his body shook, he turned his eyes to Tom. With a grimace of agony, he uttered the words, "Protect the Beasts..."

Then his body vanished, leaving a loose pile of burning green robes and a charred wizard's staff.

Aduro's apprentice had disappeared!

CHAPTER THREE

CHASING THE ENEMY

"No!" Elenna screamed.

Tom rushed forwards and stamped out the flames. There was no sign of Daltec. "You killed him!" he cried.

Kapra ignored him. "Come on, this way's quicker!" she snarled at Feldric. Seizing her wizard by the collar, Kapra lifted him wailing onto an open window ledge. The evil witch glanced back at Tom. "There are too many wizards, anyway. Only the strongest survive."

Tom ran at her, fury building in his chest. "While there's blood in my veins, I'll make you pay!"

"You'll have to catch us first," cackled Kapra, teetering on the window ledge. As Tom swung his sword, she leapt from the window, pulling Feldric behind her. Tom flung himself against the ledge and leaned out to see them drifting down through the air towards the palace walls, light as dandelion spores. Their laughter carried back to Tom's ears.

"More magic!" said Elenna grimly, craning over the ledge beside Tom.

"Who is Raksha?" Tom asked. "Aduro's never mentioned her."

"And why is she here?" Elenna murmured.

They watched as Kapra and Feldric landed softly on the ground beyond the castle walls.

"Whatever they're looking for," said Tom, "it's important enough for them to open portals from Gorgonia to Avantia."

A whine from Silver made them both spin around. One of the candlesticks in the middle of the table had sparked into life. Black smoke trailed from the flame, wrapping itself into the shape of a familiar face.

"Aduro!" gasped Elenna.

The smoke shifted as the wizard's lips moved. "I sensed danger," he said, in a voice like the whisper of wind through leaves.

"Daltec is dead," said Tom, lowering his eyes. "He tried to protect us, and we... I failed him."

"You've failed no one," said Aduro.
"My magic isn't strong enough to
stay for long. Tell me what
happened."

"A witch called Kapra is looking
for the Lake of Light," said Tom.

"Kapra!" growled Aduro. "I thought
we'd seen the last of her."

"You know her?" said Elenna.

"Kapra has always been jealous of our connection to the Beasts," said Aduro. "You must stop her."

"But the Lake of Light?" said Tom. "Surely it's just a..." He stopped as Aduro's face vanished in a wisp of smoke.

Aduro's voice travelled faintly to their ear. "Do what you can..."

"Come on!" Tom said to Elenna. "Let's go."

With Silver racing down the steps ahead of them, Tom and Elenna made their way to the stables. Storm was waiting patiently in a stall, munching hay. When he saw them his ears pricked up and he snorted.

"We need you more than ever," Tom muttered, throwing the saddle over his faithful stallion's back and fastening the bridle.

"How can we follow them?" asked Elenna, as Tom tightened the straps. "We don't even know where they're going. The Lake of Light was just a myth until now!"

Tom swung himself onto Storm's back and held out a hand for Elenna. "We'll just have to hope they've left some tracks," he said.

With Elenna in the saddle behind him, and Silver darting beside Storm's hooves, they cantered towards the main gates. Captain Harkman stood above the portcullis talking to the watchmen. It was clear he hadn't seen Kapra and Feldric leap from the window.

"Lower the drawbridge!" Tom shouted.

"In a hurry?" asked the Captain,

giving a signal for the portcullis to be lifted.

"Can you guard the palace until our return?" called Tom. His red-haired friend gave a sharp nod. Once upon a time Captain Harkman had enjoyed giving orders to Tom – now he was a faithful comrade.

The drawbridge was being lowered, but far too slowly. The chains creaked and groaned stiffly.

"We don't have time to wait!" Tom called over his shoulder to Elenna.

"Do what you have to," she said in his ear.

Spurring Storm on, they galloped up the incline of the rattling drawbridge. Tom heaved on the reins and with a *whoosh* they were airborne and Storm was leaping clear. They sailed over the swampy moat,

Silver a streak of grey fur at their side. With a bone-shaking crunch, they landed on the other side.

"Kapra and Feldric landed over there," said Elenna, pointing north.

Tom steered Storm and they charged across the fields, leaping over hedges and small streams. Tom knew that if he lost their enemies, then they might as well give up the chase. His fingers were white where they clutched the reins. *I can't let King Hugo down*, he thought. *I can't let Daltec's death be for nothing.* But the countryside all around them was deserted.

He was beginning to lose hope when they picked up tracks in the long grass.

"Thank goodness it's summer," he said, pointing at the broken stalks. The trampled grasses left a clear path; if Kapra and Feldric had been travelling over frozen mud, they wouldn't have left any clues.

He dropped Storm to a canter so they could follow the tracks carefully. But as the sun climbed to its highest point, there was still no sign of Kapra or Feldric.

"These could be deer tracks," muttered Elenna.

"We haven't seen any deer," Tom replied, trying to push his doubts away.

Storm suddenly stumbled in a rabbit hole and whinnied loudly.

"He's thrown a shoe!" said Elenna, peering down.

Just what we need! Tom thought, frustration building. Fortunately, he knew this part of Avantia well. "The village of Elderval is just over the next hill. We'll find a blacksmith there."

Not daring to push Storm hard, they dismounted and walked into the small scattering of huts and shops which nestled around a crossroads. *Every moment we waste*, he thought, *Kapra gets further out of our grasp.*

Tom heard the ring of a blacksmith's hammer across the street, and saw the sign of an anvil hanging over a shop doorway. He led Storm by the reins. Barely any of the people milling between market stalls seemed to notice them. They'd almost reached the blacksmith's door when a man in tattered clothes blocked their path. He led an old donkey fastened to a cart piled high with junk. Tom spotted rusty kettles, straw dolls, ancient cutlery. There were even items in wicker baskets hanging from the donkey's saddle. "Buying and selling!" hollered the man. "Swapping if need be!"

"We don't need anything," Tom said.

"Everyone needs something," cried the tinker. He lifted a pair of hole-riddled shoes from the cart. "A new pair of shoes, maybe?"

Elenna rolled her eyes at Tom. "No, thank you," she said.

The bedraggled man fished out
a chipped jug. "A fine piece of
crockery fit for King Hugo's table!"

Tom noticed a glinting object in the
donkey's basket. A cracked wall mirror
covered in dirty spots. *I'm surrounded
by mirrors today.* As he looked, he was
sure its surface rippled slightly. Alarm
darted through him.

"Can I buy that mirror?" he said.
"Quickly!" If it was another evil

portal, he wanted to keep it closed.

"Tom, we have to hurry," Elenna reminded him.

"A fine choice!" said the tinker. "Once owned by a queen, they say." He began to unfasten the mirror.

As he did so, they heard shouts, which seemed to come from somewhere close by – very close by. But the streets were nearly deserted!

Tom looked around, confused. The shouting grew louder – angry cries, and the clashing of metal. Elenna pulled her bow off her shoulder, her brow furrowed.

"I don't understand," she said. "It's as if the voices are coming from nowhere."

Tom took a step back as the sounds closed in on him. The tinker staggered back too, falling on his

backside, his face painted with terror.
He was looking at the mirror. The
surface bulged, and Tom realised –
That's where the shouts are coming from.
The mirror! The glassy surface seemed
to stretch and distort and a man burst
through, rolling across the dusty
ground.

Another man followed, emerging
fully formed from the cracked glass.
Then a third crashed into his back.
All three carried swords, and wore
silver talismans around their necks.
Two women tumbled from the
mirror, cursing as they dusted
themselves off. Last came a man with
scars raked across his face, carrying
a two-headed axe. He stared at Tom,
his lip curled in a sneer.

A prickle of unease ran over Tom's
body as his glance came to rest on

the talisman at the man's throat. I've
seen that before. His eyes darted back
up to the man's face as
understanding dawned.

"You're the rebels of Gorgonia!"

CHAPTER FOUR

A CALL TO FIGHT

"What of it?" snarled the scarred man, turning away. "Men, we have to find the Lake of Light. Rustle up some horses. Steal them if you have to." His glance fell on Storm. "That looks like a strong stallion."

The leader tried to push past Tom, but he caught the man's arm. "You're looking for the lake too?" he asked.

The man shook Tom's arm free and raised his axe threateningly. Tom noticed the handle ended with the same bronze embossing as Feldric's staff. Had the evil wizard summoned these soldiers?

"Why we're here is none of your business," said the rebel. "Keep your hands off me, unless you want to lose them. And keep away from things that don't concern you." His voice was heavy with threat as he brought his face close to Tom's.

"We were told you might be here. You're to keep your nose out of other people's business."

Who'd been talking to these rebels about Tom? He shared an anxious glance with Elenna.

"We should have known Kapra wouldn't just let us follow her," Elenna whispered. "It must be her and that evil wizard."

"Did Kapra summon you here?" Tom asked. "To stop us giving chase?"

Waves of shock passed over Tom. When he'd last known the rebels of Gorgonia, they'd fought on the side of good against the evil wizard Malvel. What had that witch done to them?

The tinker was climbing stiffly back to his feet. He pointed at the mirror. "I don't understand. How can people come out of there?"

Milo hoisted his axe across his shoulder and guffawed. "Haven't you heard of portals, old fool?"

"Please," Tom tried again, "you shouldn't be here. Kapra must have an evil hold over you."

With a roar, the rebel leader kicked Tom in the chest, sending him sprawling on the dusty ground.

"Don't tell us what we should be doing!" he snarled.

Elenna ran to help Tom stand. He was winded and, for a moment, struggled to draw breath into his lungs.

"You animals!" Elenna spat. Her hand moved to her quiver of arrows, but Tom shook his head. The pain in his lungs was fading away. He advanced a pace on Milo, who grinned.

"You tell your friend to put her arrows away," he said. "But I'd like to see your sword. Let's finish this." He swung the axe in an arc in front of him. "Fight me, boy! I could use some practice."

Tom shook his head. "I don't fight unless I have to. Is this what Kapra's done to you? When I knew the rebels of old, you fought on the side of good – you didn't challenge strangers to sword fights."

Milo grimaced and swung the axe a finger's width from the tinker's neck. The old man's eyes widened and his lip quivered. "One more word from you, boy, and he's going to lose his head," the rebel leader spat. "Get your sword out and fight me!"

What choice do I have? Tom thought, glancing at the tinker's terrified face. *I won't see an innocent man cut down.* "Very well," said Tom, drawing his sword, and shrugging his shield onto his arm.

Milo released the man, kicking him over towards his cart. Tom and the rebel leader circled one another, with Elenna and the others crowding around them.

"Be careful, Tom!" Elenna called.

Tom was already wondering how he could end this fight without killing the rebel leader. *I don't want his blood on my hands*, he thought.

Milo lunged with an overarm swing that Tom took on his shield. The thud jarred his shoulder, sending a wave of pain along his arm. He swiped with the flat of his sword, catching the rebel leader across the thigh. The man crumpled with a groan. One of the other rebels rushed forwards gripping a rapier, but Milo waved him back. "Leave him to me," he growled.

Tom knew he could have called on the powers of his shield, but he wanted this to be a fair fight.

Hobbling to his feet, the man hacked again. Tom leapt aside and

the axehead lodged in the ground.
Tom slid his sword under the rebel
leader's chin, the point of his blade
caressing the man's throat. It was
a hollow victory. "It's over," he said.

Breathing heavily, Milo nodded.
"Beaten fairly," he muttered.

Tom withdrew his sword, and
half-turned to Elenna. As he did so,
he saw the blur of a fist, and Milo

punched him in the jaw. The world seemed to spin, and he felt himself falling. He landed awkwardly in a cloud of dust.

"I'll let you keep your life," said the rebel, standing over him, "but I'll take this as spoils." Through his double vision, Tom saw Milo gripping his shield. "No..." he mumbled.

Then he heard a panicked snorting from Storm. He tried to get to his feet, but his head swam and vision blurred. He fell back down in the dirt.

They were trying to steal Tom's horse!

CHAPTER FIVE

A GOLDEN HOOK

"Get off him!" Elenna shouted. Tom tried again to struggle up. Storm was rearing up as two Gorgonians lunged to grab his reins. He kicked a hoof at one of the men, sending him reeling into the arms of a comrade. *Good old Storm*, Tom managed to think through the haze that filled his head. He saw Elenna aim an arrow at the other man, who backed off. "Keep your nag!" he said.

There was a high, thin whistle and the rebels turned to race away. As they retreated they laughed and called to each other. Tom sat up on his elbows and watched them leave, waiting for the pain to subside. Elenna ran and helped him sit up properly.

"We have to go after them," said Tom, trying to stand. His legs felt like jelly and his vision swam.

"You can't," said Elenna. "Sit here a moment."

Tom waited for his senses to return. In the distance he heard the stampeding of hooves. The rebels had found other horses to steal.

"I've lost my shield," he said at last, a mixture of anger and despair clawing at his insides.

"We'll get it back," said Elenna.

"We just have to fix Storm's shoe and find the Lake of Light."

Tom massaged his jaw. "Is that all? It feels as though everything's against us. Storm losing a shoe, the rebels getting in our way... I'm meant to be protecting Avantia and I'm sitting in the dirt, winded by a Gorgonian rebel!"

"I thought you were a hero! Is this how heroes talk? Come on, you can

at least get up." Elenna helped him to his feet.

Nothing felt right without the shield on his back. As he stroked Storm's nose, he heard the tinker muttering something behind the cart. It sounded like: "Lake of Light... I didn't think anyone else knew it was real."

Tom went to him, but the tinker was still staring at the mirror. "What do you know of the Lake of Light?" he asked.

The tinker shrugged and held out an open palm. "What's the information worth?"

"I don't have anything..." he said.

"I do," said Elenna. Tom looked at her, surprised. She reached into the bottom of her quiver and pulled out a golden fish hook. "I bought this on

my last visit to my uncle," she said, holding the hook out between her finger and thumb. "It's supposed to catch even the most wily fish."

The tinker's eyes flashed greedily. "Very nice!" he said, reaching out.

Elenna snapped her hand closed. "Information first."

"All right," said the tinker glumly. As Tom led Storm to the blacksmith's, the tinker began to talk. "The Lake of Light is in the Lost Valley. It only appears at sundown at the height of summer, when the heat waves coming off the cornfields part to reveal a secret place. The valley lies where the Central Plains meet the Forest of Fear. But remember, it only appears at sunset. Get there too late and you'll be disappointed."

Tom looked into the sky, and saw the sun was already well past its highest point. "We don't have any time to lose," he said to Elenna. "Let's get Storm's shoe fitted."

The tinker held out his hand. "Aren't you forgetting something?"

Elenna handed over the golden fish hook. The tinker grinned and held it up to the light. "Nice doing business with you," he said. As he patted his donkey's neck, his smile vanished. "There's one more thing I'll tell you," he said. "And this is for free. They say a monster lurks in the Lake of

Light, a creature terrible to behold. People call him 'Raksha'." He waved a hand carelessly. "But it's probably just a silly story, isn't it?"

"Probably," Tom muttered, sharing a worried glance with Elenna. Kapra had said they needed the Mirror of Raksha once they reached the lake.

Raksha, he thought. *Am I about to face another Beast?*

CHAPTER SIX

A VISION EMERGES

Tom urged Storm forwards and the stallion galloped even faster. They were nearing the western edge of the Forest of Fear.

The village blacksmith had nailed a new shoe to Storm's hoof, working almost as quickly as Uncle Henry.

"There's no time to waste," Tom had said, climbing into the saddle. Without a word, Elenna had scrambled up behind them and Storm had taken off straight away, with Silver following. So far, there hadn't been any sign of the evil wizard and witch other than their tracks and now Tom's nerves were strung tight.

He had to get to the valley before dusk. Two kingdoms depended on him – Avantia and Gorgonia. Taladon was in Gorgonia. *What's my father doing over there?* Tom wondered. *Why hadn't he stopped the rebels from forcing their way into Avantia?*

"What are you thinking?" Elenna asked, concern filling her voice.

Tom shook the dark thoughts out of his head. "I'm just wondering why we haven't... I mean, what are..."

"You're thinking about Taladon and Aduro, aren't you?" Elenna murmured. "I've been thinking the same things. What are they doing in

70

Gorgonia? And what of King Hugo?"

"We'll find out in good time," Tom said, forcing himself to sound more confident than he felt. "For now, we must do what we can."

"Agreed!" Elenna cried. "Come on, Silver!"

Tom dug his heels into Storm's flanks, and they galloped faster than ever, with Elenna's wolf running by their side.

They rode along a track around the edge of the Forest of Fear. Soon Tom's legs ached from gripping Storm's flanks for so long.

They reached the place where the forest met the Central Plains. Tom surveyed the pasture that spread as far as the horizon.

"This is the place," he said, "but where's the Lost Valley?"

Elenna shrugged and stared towards the setting sun, which hovered just above the horizon. "I know where I can get a better view." She went to a tree, and began to climb into the lower branches.

Tom stared west until his eyes hurt. The dying sun cast rays of red and gold light through the thin wisps of cloud. "Nothing!" he said. "That tinker must have lied to us. I knew there was something odd about him. I shouldn't have trusted..."

"Over there!" Elenna shouted.

She pointed over Tom's head and he followed the line of her finger. Sure enough, in the wavering light of the plains, he saw a patch of vivid green.

"It must be the Lost Valley!" said Elenna, scrambling down.

Silver howled as Tom urged Storm into a trot. The ground dipped, but Tom kept the stallion cantering in a straight line. They found a narrow path leading up towards a mound. Tom could feel his skin tingling with anticipation as they reached the top.

Elenna gasped. Tom drew in the reins, bringing Storm to a halt. The sun was half gone already, leaving just a glowing pink orb on the

horizon. But the sight beneath them
was even more spectacular.

A steep-sided valley, partly covered

with trees and boulders, fell away
to a circular pool. It shimmered like
a giant, polished mirror, at least three
hundred paces wide, but the light
seemed to come from within. It
glowed like a full moon. Tom didn't
think he'd ever seen anything so
magical.

"We've found the Lake of Light!"
he cried.

CHAPTER SEVEN

AN OLD FOE

Tom climbed out of the saddle and led Storm slowly, the horse scattering rocks into the steep-sided valley with his hooves. Silver picked his way confidently down with Elenna at his side.

They were almost at the bottom, near the perfectly still water, when Tom saw figures in the shadows on the far side.

"Kapra and Feldric," he muttered.

Their two enemies stood at the
shore of the lake. Tom could just see
the wizard holding aloft the Mirror
of Raksha. It glinted in his hand,
catching the last of the sun's rays and
reflecting them onto the water's
surface. Kapra's voice carried eerily
in the creeping dusk.

Strength of Six, Lake of Light,
Summon Raksha, help us fight."

Elenna threw Tom a confused

glance. "What's the 'strength of six'?" she asked.

The witch of Gorgonia repeated the chant, loud and shrill this time. The ground began to rumble beneath their feet, and the surface of the lake rippled. A silhouette appeared on the ridge above the valley. At first, Tom couldn't be sure what he was seeing. It looked like a rider on the back of a giant horse. Then he understood.

"That's Tagus!" he gasped.

The Horse-Man of the plains galloped into the valley, his mighty human chest rising and falling with heavy breaths.

I think I know what the 'strength of six' means... Tom thought.

Another shape swept over their heads, glowing red. It was Epos, lit by the embers blazing in her gliding wings.

The Flame Bird landed at the side of the lake, her bronze beak scattering light, her talons gripping rock.

"I don't believe it. Kapra's summoning the Good Beasts of Avantia," Tom said.

"Daltec warned us..." Elenna said.

The ground shook again with rhythmic shocks. Nanook appeared, red eyes glowing. Her white hair looked almost silver as she pounded down the valleyside. A screech made Tom look up, as the black shape of Ferno the Fire Dragon sailed through the sky, his scales darkly menacing and flames dripping from his mouth.

A shape emerged from the surface of the lake near to Tom and Sepron poked his head through the water, trailing weeds from his razor-sharp jaws. Finally, Arcta leapt over the

ridge, sliding down towards Kapra
and Feldric. When he reached the
lake's edge, he pounded his shaggy
chest and roared.

Tom watched as the six Beasts arranged themselves in a circle around the lake. Normally seeing his old friends together would have filled him with joy, but it was clear something was very wrong. Each Beast had their eyes fixed on the Mirror of Raksha in Feldric's hand. They didn't even glance at Tom.

"Can't you stop them?" asked Elenna desperately.

Tom closed his eyes and concentrated on the power of the ruby jewel in his belt, won from Torgor the Minotaur. It gave him the power to communicate with the Beasts. He reached out with his mind, but pain spiked through his head.

"It's not working," he said. "Kapra's brainwashed them!"

"Then we have to stop Feldric," said

Elenna. "The mirror must be the key! We have to get it from him."

Tom seized Storm's reins and mounted, letting Elenna jump up behind him. They cantered down towards the lake, picking their way around the scattered boulders towards Kapra and Feldric.

Tom heard a sudden whistle in the air, and felt a stinging pain in his leg. Storm snorted and reared, throwing them clear. Tom landed in a heap on the ground, his elbows jarring painfully against shingle. Silver yelped too, writhing on the ground.

"What happened?" asked Elenna, getting to her feet. "Oh, Silver!"

Tom climbed stiffly up. The wolf's fur was matted with blood. He went to Storm and rubbed the flat of his hand over his glossy coat – the stallion's flank was the same. Looking closer, he saw several pieces of sharp flint embedded in Storm's side. Glancing down, Tom saw a trickle of blood down his thigh.

"Someone attacked us!" he said, pulling the bloodied shard free.

"Not just someone!" called a familiar voice. "Your old friend!"

Tom and Elenna spun round together. Petra emerged from some bushes, and hopped up onto a boulder, a sling dangling from her hand.

"Sorry if I hurt your pathetic pets," she giggled.

"You'll suffer for that," said Elenna, reaching for an arrow.

Petra lifted her sling in warning. "I wouldn't if I were you. My aim's good enough to take out both your eyes."

"What's the matter with you?"

asked Tom. "Do you want to see
Avantia brought to its knees?" First
Storm losing a shoe and now this.
Tom had to get to Feldric and Kapra!
He had to stop them, before they cast
more of a spell over the six Beasts.

"You've met my mother then?" said
Petra. "I thought I'd come along and
join the fun."

"She'll turn the Good Beasts to bad," said Elenna. "Without their protection, Avantia is doomed."

"You might not see eye to eye with us," Tom urged, "but this is the only home you know!"

Petra's smile faded a little, and her lip twisted cruelly. "I love my mother a lot more than this place," she said. "Why should I care what happens to your kingdom?"

Tom cast a glance over to the lake. Kapra was still chanting. Now, the good Beasts stood like statues at the water's edge. "Were you in on the plan all along?" he asked, watching Petra carefully. Sure enough, her pudgy cheeks began to colour.

"I didn't think so," Tom said, folding his arms. For the first time in his life, he felt sorry for the little witch.

"It doesn't have to be like this, Petra. Help us – we'll show you more gratitude than your mother."

"You may love her," Elenna added, "but the feeling is one-way, Petra. I know what it's like to be without parents, alive or dead. It hurts, doesn't it?"

"What do you mean?" asked the girl witch, with a nervous laugh. "I don't know what you're talking about." Her smile fell away and her voice turned high and shrill. "My mother loves me!"

"She called you a wretch," Elenna told her. "We heard her with our own ears."

Petra started the sling swinging. "You're lying."

"A snivelling wretch'," Tom added. By the lake, Feldric had added his voice to the chant. What were they doing? Tom had to find out – quickly. "Look, Petra, you don't have to do her bidding. You're stronger than her."

As Petra lowered the sling, Tom hastily checked Storm's wounds, pulling the pieces of flint carefully from the stallion's flank. How much damage had the little witch done? The wounds were superficial, but his horse must be in pain. *If only I had my shield*, Tom thought. *Epos's talon would heal these cuts.*

"She's always cruel to me," admitted Petra, looking at her feet. She nodded to Storm. "Is your horse all right?" she asked guiltily.

"You're not a monster," said Tom, pushing his advantage. He could tell Petra was weakening. "Even if your mother is."

"Show her you're not at her beck and call," added Elenna.

Petra brushed her greasy locks away from her face. She went to sit, hunched, on a boulder. "Go on, then," she said. "Do what you must. I won't stop you. I'll guard this side of the lake – I won't let her get you from over here. Now, get out of my sight before I change my mind!"

"Thank you," said Tom, as he mounted Storm. *Now we can do what we came here to do – vanquish Kapra.*

Elenna finished tending to Silver and mounted too. "Let's finish this," she said, as though reading Tom's thoughts.

He spurred Storm towards the lake, knowing that he'd do whatever it took to save Avantia. Even if it meant doing battle with the good Beasts.

CHAPTER EIGHT

FACING THE MIRROR DEMON

They galloped around the edge of the lake, past Sepron and Arcta. Neither Beast even turned their head to look. They stared, transfixed by the mirror Feldric held.

"Fight it!" Tom shouted. "Don't sucuumb!"

The wizard grinned and raised the mirror higher, his arm straight up to catch the the last rays of light. Kapra intoned, *"Strength of Six, Lake of Light..."* She broke off when she saw them coming. "Here at last!" she cackled. She pulled the green pendant from her robes. At once, snakes fell from her head and writhed across the ground towards them. Tom slid from the saddle, drawing his sword. "Take Storm out of the way!" he called to Elenna. The horse was already neighing nervously at the sight of the snakes.

Elenna gave a curt nod and gripped the reins, wheeling the stallion around to the safety of several boulders. Tom faced the snakes, which were pulsing across the ground with flickering tongues. There were more than he could count! He swung his sword at the first, slicing it in two. But the tail sprouted another head. Both snakes

writhed up his legs, hissing fiercely as their beady eyes glinted. He shook one free, but the other slipped under his tunic and slithered up his torso. He thrashed around, while two other snakes leapt up. Fangs gripped his wrist, puncturing the skin, and more caught his thigh. There was a pain like hot needles sinking into his flesh! A snake coiled around his neck and began to tighten. He felt his throat constrict.

"Get off me!" Tom croaked. He fell to the ground, rolling over to free himself. With an almighty effort, he tore the viper loose from his throat before it choked him, casting it aside.

Panting and panicked, he retreated to where Elenna sheltered with Storm. The snakes slithered back to Kapra, who called a taunt. "Be warned, Avantian! Keep out of this business, or meet your end!"

A whisper from behind them drew Tom's attention. Looking over his shoulder, he saw shapes moving in the woodland area up the slope. A chill gripped his heart when he realised who it was. Milo and his Gorgonian rebels stood at the treeline. Several men held fast

innocent Avantians, with daggers at
their throats. What were the rebels
doing now? Why were they attacking
people? Tom quickly scanned the
group for a glimpse of his shield, but
it was nowhere to be seen. *What have
they done with it?*

"I wouldn't interfere, if I were
you," called Milo. "The lives of these

people depend upon Kapra getting her way."

"They dragged us from our farms," said one of the captives. "Please, do as they say."

Feldric reached up on the tips of his toes, angling the last ray of the sun onto the water. From the middle of the lake, where the mirror reflected the light, a bubble emerged.

"Something's alive down there," muttered Elenna. Tom felt her hand grip his arm, and Silver whined.

Another bubble trickled to the surface and burst. Around the lake, the six good Beasts burst into life, filling the air with the sound of their howls, roars and cries. Nanook pounded the ground with her fists. Epos shrieked, swiping her flame-covered wings. Sepron spewed water

spray over the lake, which hissed as it came into contact with a spurt of fire from Ferno. Arcta stamped in the shallows, throwing up huge waves.

"Whatever's happening, they're adding their power," Tom muttered. He could see that the Beasts were drawing on all their strength.

"By the power of six, Raksha the Mirror Demon is summoned!" shrieked Kapra.

A huge silhouette grew beneath

the lake and more bubbles spread
across the water. The surface broke,
cascading spray over Tom and Elenna
and making Storm neigh in fear.

With water pouring from its sides,
a huge creature emerged. With a
shudder of dread, Tom knew
immediately what it was: a Beast.

He'd never seen anything like this.
Raksha's head was lined with thick
coiling serpents to match Kapra's.
He reared up on impossibly tall hind
legs. Mighty arms beat his chest,
making the trees shake and stones
scatter down the valleyside.

Through his shock, Tom realised
there was something familiar about
the Beast. "Wait a moment..." he
muttered.

Raksha's hands ended in black
claws just like Ferno's, and between

them Raksha rolled a fireball similar to those Epos could form. His feet, shaped like Tagus's hooves, stood planted in the water, and his chest was covered in shaggy pale hair like Nanook's. His legs glistened with a sea serpent's scales. Finally, one mad eye gleamed in the centre of his forehead. *Like Arcta...* Tom thought.

"He's a combination of all the good Beasts!" he cried.

A coat of thick metal armour covered much of the Beast's body.

"Tom, your shield!" gasped Elenna.

There, locked in the centre of Raksha's breastplate and larger than it had ever been, was Tom's shield.

"That must be how he's controlling the Beasts," he said. "The rebels handed my shield over to Kapra." He'd never felt so betrayed.

He leapt onto a boulder, and aimed his sword at the Mirror Demon. "That belongs to me!" he called.

Raksha threw back his head and roared with fury, then trained his single eye on Tom.

"The Mirror Demon has the strength of six Beasts," crowed Kapra. "He'll kill anyone in his path! And Raksha is mine. Now I'm the most powerful witch in all the kingdoms! I can take this evil magic anywhere."

She pointed over their shoulders and Tom saw the air behind him had torn open. In the middle of a swirl of yellow smoke, stood a bald, thin man, robes swirling.

"It's Kerlo, the Gatekeeper of Gorgonia!" said Elenna.

The Gatekeeper pointed his staff angrily at Kapra. "You cannot open

portals at will, witch-fiend."

"Care to stop me?" chuckled Kapra.

Tom heard another roar and
Raksha emerged from the lake,
driving huge waves of water which
knocked them off their feet. Tom
slammed into the mud and the Beast
pounded towards them on giant
hooves. Tom had only half drawn his
sword when one of the Beast's
massive talons seized him around the

middle and lifted him into the air. With lightning speed, the Mirror Demon swooped to grip a screaming Elenna in his other hand, and brought each of them level with his unblinking black eye. Tom writhed desperately but couldn't free himself.

He's going to crush the life out of us!

"Time for a little trip!" laughed Kapra.

Storm reared at Raksha's hooves, and Silver yelped and snapped.

"Stay back!" Elenna shouted.

Tom felt himself flung towards the portal. He heard Elenna cry out in fear. Strange energy thrummed through all his limbs, making his whole body shudder, and then with a blinding flash of light Avantia disappeared.

Would Tom ever see his home again?

STORY TWO

Tom's preening arrogance has got the better of him. He thought he could take on Kapra and myself. He was wrong! Now, we have banished him and Elenna to Gorgonia!

Raksha is Kapra's creature and has the strength of six Beasts – which gives my mistress power to send her evil to any kingdom and ruin Avantia in the process.

Tom is trapped in an alien kingdom and his father is nowhere to be seen. Can a single boy overcome this? Unlikely. I don't have the strength to resist Kapra's plans – how can Tom possibly hope to do what a wizard can't?

Yours, the new wizard of Avantia

Feldric

CHAPTER ONE

FAR FROM HOME

Tom landed with a thud on hard, dusty ground. He smelled burning – his hair was singed! Elenna groaned beside him. Rolling over, Tom opened his eyes onto a swirling red sky. He was surrounded by boulders that were strewn across a bleak desert landscape. The only sign of life was a few dying tree trunks scattered over the rolling plain.

"Gorgonia..." he murmured.

"Indeed, young man," said a deep voice.

Tom scrambled to his feet, and saw Kerlo standing beside him. Elenna stood up too and looked around.

"Tom, the portal!" she cried.

Just a few paces away, beside a filthy expanse of water the same size as the Lake of Light, was a rift in the air identical to the one they'd been hurled through in Avantia.

"We need to get back and stop Kapra!" said Tom.

Lightning flashed across the Gorgonian sky, and Tom heard shouts and the clashing of weapons.

"Move it!" someone yelled.

He turned full circle, but he couldn't see where the sounds were coming from. Then, from the centre of the portal, a farmer from Avantia

emerged, blinking in terror. Another
followed, then a whole group. With
angry calls, armed Gorgonian rebels
leapt through the portal after them,
led by Milo.

"Where have you brought us?"
asked an Avantian woman. She

pointed at the portal. "What is that thing?"

The rebels shoved the Avantians into a huddle. Tom recognised them as the people who'd been kidnapped. The portal snapped shut behind them.

"Welcome to our home!" sneered Milo.

Tom shook his head slowly, trying to take it all in. He was stranded in Gorgonia and back there, in Avantia, who knew what Raksha would do under the thrall of Kapra?

"Keep moving!" shouted the leader of the rebels.

An Avantian shepherd swung his staff, but only managed to strike a rebel's arm.

"You'll pay for that!" shouted the Gorgonian, lifting a spiked mace over his head.

Tom leapt forward, shoving the Avantian out of harm's way and kicking the rebel soldier in the gut. He doubled over with an *oomph*. Two more Gorgonians closed on Tom, but Elenna leapt to his side, arrow at the ready. "Take another step, and you'll die!" she said.

"You stole my shield and gave it to Kapra!" Tom spluttered, as he waited for the pain in his stomach to fade.

The leader of the rebels took
a menacing step forwards.

"Enough!" bellowed Kerlo.

"Out of the way, old man," called
Milo. "This doesn't concern you."

Kerlo pointed a long finger at the
leader's face. "I am the Gatekeeper
between the worlds!" he said.
"Would you dare strike a blow
against me? Has Kapra made you
bad to the core?"

To Tom's surprise, Milo hesitated
then lowered his axe, and the other
rebels did the same. A shadow of
guilt passed over his face, and he
rubbed his brow as though he was
trying to remember who he was.

"I won't stand by and allow
bloodshed," said Kerlo. "You've
brought these people here against
their will. Now, go!"

"It was that woman," Milo mumbled, shaking his head. "She had some sort of hold over us." He gave his head a final shake then looked up at Tom, his face white with shock. "What did we do back there? You have to tell me!" The other rebels shared confused glances, some of them staggering slightly. It looked as though they were finally emerging from Kapra's thrall.

"Don't worry about it," Tom said. "There's nothing you can do about it now."

Milo looked at Tom's empty arm. "Your shield. Where is it?"

"The Beast has it," Elenna told him, her face clouded with anger.

"Leave us now," Kerlo told the rebels.

Milo hesitated, then led the

Gorgonian rebels away. Soon Tom was watching their backs disappear over the horizon. They'd done more harm than they could possibly imagine, but it wasn't their fault.

Tom faced the space where the portal had been again. "We have to get home."

"Hold on. We've bigger problems," said Elenna. She was standing at the rim of the Gorgonian lake. Green slime coated the water, but at the centre, Tom saw bubbles breaking the stinking surface. The water that was almost a mirror image of the Lake of Light...

Understanding spread through Tom. "Get back!" he shouted, waving a hand. "Raksha's coming."

As the farmers stumbled away from the water's edge, the Mirror Demon burst from the depths, his armour glittering with spray. Spreading his arms, Tom saw he gripped a fireball in his claws. He turned his shaggy head towards them, then hurled the flaming orb. It streaked towards them, trailing fire, and Tom had to tackle a farmer out of its path. The fireball exploded in sparks over the

ground and Tom felt heat bake the
side of his face.

"We have to hide!" said Elenna.

Kerlo beckoned them towards him.
"I know a place. Quickly!"

A second fireball streaked over
his head, lighting up the landscape
as it smashed into the ground ahead
of them.

Tom followed as Kerlo and Elenna led the Avantians up the hill, sheltering among boulders as they ran. Tom looked desperately around him – where was his father? Taladon was meant to be in Gorgonia! Behind them, Raksha tore the air with his claws and let out a ferocious roar.

"This way!" said Kerlo.

Tom saw now where he was leading them. The hillside opened up in a jagged crevasse, just wide enough for them to squeeze through one at a time. While Kerlo ushered the Avantian farmers inside, Tom saw Raksha step out of the water, mighty chest heaving and hooves stamping the ground.

I have to stop him, he thought. *But how?*

Raksha bounded up the slope

towards them, taking huge strides and swinging his claws. Elenna squeezed through the gap after Kerlo. "Tom, come on!" she cried.

Raksha's eye gleamed with anger as he closed in. Tom was vulnerable without his shield. *I can't face him yet – I need a plan.* Elenna's fingers gripped his arm and he allowed her to pull him through the gap to safety where the Avantians huddled together in near-darkness.

Raksha smashed his fists against the cave entrance, bringing down cascades of dust. His roars filled the tiny cavern, and he managed to push one claw inside. Tom and the others pressed against the back wall as the claw slashed the air. After a few moments, Raksha gave up and they felt his stamping rock the ground as he retreated.

"I've never run away from a Beast before," said Tom, staring at his feet.

"You did the right thing," said Kerlo. "Raksha has the power of six Beasts – he's invincible."

"That's it!" said Tom. He rushed to the crack, and looked out. Raksha was beating his chest in triumph back near the lake. In the centre of his chest the tokens on Tom's shield shone like lanterns.

"What?" asked Elenna.

"The shield must give the Beast his powers," said Tom. "Remember how I first liberated the Beasts?"

"You took the tokens," said Elenna, "and embedded them in the shield." Her face lit up as she seemed to catch on to Tom's thinking. "The shield is what helped bring Raksha to life."

"Exactly! If I can take the tokens out again, the Mirror Demon will lose his power. We need to lure him back to Avantia, and rob him of his magic."

Kerlo pointed a bony finger

through the gap. "But the portal..." he said.

Tom remembered: the portal had snapped shut after the Avantians.

We're trapped here, Tom realised as the people in the cave began murmuring unhappily. *I've let the Good Beasts down.*

CHAPTER TWO

HOPE ON A KNIFE EDGE

"No, Tom – look! There's...something there." Elenna pointed. Raksha was crashing through the lake, throwing up sheets of water.

"I can't see anything," said Tom.

"Beside that dead tree," said Elenna. "Look carefully."

Sure enough, Tom saw it. Floating in the air, where the portal had been, was an almost invisible line. It looked like a heat haze, blurring the sky.

"It's like the portal hasn't sealed properly," said Tom.

"Sometimes gateways leave a seam," said Kerlo. "But I know of no spell that can open them again."

"I think I can help," said a voice.

Tom turned to see a pair of eyes in the darkness. One of the Avantians, an old grizzled farmer, stepped forward. "You could use this."

He held a small knife, barely big enough to peel a piece of fruit.

"I'm grateful," said Tom, "but

I don't think it will help."

"No, listen," said the man, holding out the blade. "This knife has special powers."

"Magic?" said Elenna, taking it, and turning it over in her hands. Its blade was thin, and rusty. She tested it on the edge of her tunic and rolled her eyes. "It's not even sharp."

But as she handed it to Tom, he felt a strange sensation shiver up his arm. He glanced at Elenna.

"You think we should trust this man?" she whispered.

"We don't have a choice," said Tom.

"Let me try to open the portal," said Elenna, taking back the knife. "I'm good with a dagger." As she clutched it, the blade glowed pale blue. "It's working!"

Tom was proud of his friend's

bravery, but he couldn't let her go alone. "I'll distract Raksha," he said. He turned to the crowd of frightened Avantians. "You have to be ready. If Elenna manages to open the portal again, we'll have to make a run for it."

The farmers nodded anxiously, clutching at each other. Elenna was waiting by the crack. It was time. Tom drew his sword and stepped out.

Raksha didn't see him at first. The Beast was facing the other way, bellowing at the swirling scarlet clouds above. Tom picked up a piece of baked rock from the ground, and drew back his arm.

"Over here, Raksha!" Tom yelled, as he threw the rock.

The rock smashed on the back of Raksha's armour. The Beast swivelled, and all the snakes' heads turned in

Tom's direction. The giant dark pool
of Raksha's eye flashed as he let out
a roar. In three mighty strides, the
Mirror Demon reached the edge of the
water and bounded towards the cave.

Tom sprinted away, leaping over
boulders, and the earth shook as the
Beast pursued him. When he turned,
Raksha was bearing down on him,
claws scraping sparks off the ground.
But behind him, Elenna sprinted
along the bank of the lake towards
the barely visible seam in the air.

Hurry! Tom willed her. He dived and rolled as Raksha brought down a huge hoof. Cracks splintered through the hard packed earth.

The Beast stood over him, and the tokens in the shield glowed with power. But Raksha was no longer looking at him. He'd spotted Elenna, and before Tom could act, he was running towards her. In one huge hand a fireball sparked into life.

"Look out!" Tom yelled. Elenna turned just in time to see the ball of flame shooting through the air. She ducked and the fireball plunged into the lake, sizzling the water to boiling point. Elenna came up, spluttering, but Raksha had already reached her, aiming a deadly kick. She dodged, and managed to throw her arms around Raksha's armoured leg.

The Beast thrashed and roared, trying to kick her loose, but Elenna held on.

Tom ran towards the lake as fast as he could. Finally, with a growl, Raksha plucked Elenna from his leg with a talon, slicing through her tunic. He threw her high into the air.

Tom was sure that he was about to see his friend broken on the rocks.

"Elenna!"

CHAPTER THREE

A CHINK IN THE ARMOUR

Elenna twisted, and flung out a hand holding the knife. Suddenly she stopped, as if caught by an invisible string.

She's found the seam! Tom realised. The blade of the knife had caught it, suspending her in mid-air as she clung on.

Slowly, Elenna slid down, and the knife sliced through the portal, tearing it open as she dropped safely to the ground. She turned back to the cave. "Quickly, all of you!" she shouted.

"Run!" Tom called. As the first Avantian clambered out of the crack in the rock, Tom darted up behind Raksha. He slashed his sword across the back of the Beast's unarmoured heel, and the Mirror Demon bellowed in pain and fury. He swiped back and forth with his claws, trying to snatch Tom up. Tom used his best footwork to avoid the raking talons, stepping backwards to draw the Beast towards him. He noticed the steady stream of Avantians heading for the portal where Elenna waited. *At least they'll be safe*, he just had time to think.

Then he tripped over a loose rock,

and landed beneath the Beast.
Raksha reached for him with a claw,
and Tom swung his sword, catching
the dagger-like talons a hand's width
from his face. He scrambled up, and
ran between the Beast's legs. Elenna
was half in the portal already,
beckoning to him.

"He's right behind you!" she called.

Tom pumped his arms for more speed, but he could feel the Mirror Demon's breath on his back. With a last surge of speed, he leapt for the narrow portal.

For a heartbeat, all went dark. His skin felt hot and cold at the same time, and energy fizzed through his bones. Then he slid over grassy ground.

I'm home!

He scrambled to his feet as a set of claws burst through the portal beside his head. Then a second set. He heard the distant echoes of roaring.

"Raksha's too big to follow us through!" said Elenna. "Even a Beast isn't powerful enough to tear open the portal."

A moment later, the claws

vanished. *He's given up*, Tom thought. But then he remembered the lake – Raksha could come crashing through the water at any moment.

"Back so soon?" a cackling voice called.

At the edge of the lake, Kapra and Feldric stood, surrounded by the six Good Beasts of Avantia. The Witch of Gorgonia was holding her green

pendant. Snakes slithered over the
bodies of the Beasts. From the way
their bodies hung heavy, and their
eyes stared glassily, it looked as
though they were being drained

of power. Sepron could barely keep his sagging head above the water, while Nanook leant against Arcta. Ferno had wrapped his wings tight to his body, and no flames flickered over Epos's pinions. Tagus lay, collapsed on his side.

"Release them!" Tom shouted. He needed them to help him fight.

Too late: Raksha burst up from the centre of the lake, scattering droplets from his shaggy head. He reached to the sky with his arms, opening his jaws with a colossal roar.

"Quick," Tom said the Avantians. "Train your weapons on the witch and her helper. Don't let them escape. I'll tackle Raksha."

"What are you going to do?" asked Elenna.

Tom looked up at Raksha. Storm

and Silver were doing their best to distract the Beast, galloping and darting in and out of range, tempting the Mirror Demon out of the lake. But Tom's eyes were on his shield in the centre of the Beast's armour.

"I'm going to get those tokens back," he said. "Give me the dagger."

Elenna handed it to him with a puzzled frown, as the Avantians cautiously approached Kapra and Feldric. The witch laughed and thrust the pendant towards them. More snakes dropped from her head, slithering to form a hissing wall between her and the brave farmers. "Stay back!" Kapra warned.

Tom tucked the dagger in his waistband. *I have to get to the shield!* With the Beast reaching out for Elenna's darting wolf, Tom held his

breath and dived under the surface of the lake. With powerful strokes, he swam through the murky water until he reached the trunk-like legs of the Beast. He broke the surface right beneath Raksha's massive body. Luckily, the Beast still hadn't seen him.

Tom tried to catch one of the plates of Raskha's leg armour but it seemed to be covered in oily slime, and he slid off helplessly. It must have been the gunge from the Gorgonian lake. There was only one other way.

As Raksha lunged for Silver, who nimbly sprang clear, Tom managed to squeeze underneath the stiff, toughened leather, between the armour and Raksha's scaled leg. It was almost suffocating, but Tom would have to use small, shallow breaths. "While there's blood in my veins," he muttered, "I won't stop."

Raksha must have felt something, because he began to thrash around. Tom's head snapped back, striking the armour and then the Beast's shin. Lights danced in front of his eyes as he struggled to stay conscious. Then he started to climb, gripping the Beast's scales and pulling himself up in the confined space.

The heat was unbearable and
a rotten stench filled his nostrils.
Through the armour, he heard
Silver's howls as the wolf tried to
draw Raksha's attention. Tom was
pouring with sweat by the time he

reached the Beast's heaving chest. He could see dimly, thanks to the light that crept around the edges of the breastplate. He'd arrived at the back of his shield. By some magic, the shield had grown to five or six times its normal size, and he could see the outline of the tokens embedded in the front. He made out the shape of Epos's talon. Tom managed to draw his dagger, the blade still shining blue, and began scraping away at the wood behind the talon. It was easier to work with a short, stubby dagger than with his sword in this space.

A thud shook the teeth in Tom's head, then another. He realised Raksha must be punching his own chest, trying to shake him loose.

He braced his feet against the giant

talon outline. With all his strength, he pushed against the back of the shield. "You can rage all you want," he muttered. "I'm not going anywhere!"

CHAPTER FOUR

TIPPING THE ODDS

Tom gritted his teeth and pushed. The muscles of his legs burned, but the wood of the shield bent and splintered. Then, with a crack, it gave way and the talon burst free of the surface. Raksha roared with pain and Tom peered out through the jagged hole that was left.

The talon spiralled through the air and landed in the lake with a splash.

"Tom, you did it!" Elenna shouted.

As soon as she'd spoken, Epos cawed with delight and spread her wings, throwing off the snakes that plagued her. The Flame Bird leapt into the air, fire surging across her feathers, and swooped over Raksha's head. As Raksha flailed at her, she darted through the air and stabbed at his one eye with her hooked, golden beak. The Mirror Demon writhed and groaned.

"Fight them, Raksha!" Kapra screamed.

Tom punched a sharp splinter away, and climbed through the hole onto the outside of the shield. Gripping the edge with one hand, he used the dagger to hack at the wood around Sepron's fang. It took half a dozen hacks from the dagger before

Sepron's tooth fell free, following the talon into the lake.

As soon as the token hit the surface, the Sea Serpent lifted his head on his powerful, shimmering neck, and plunged beneath the waves. A wall of water showered

down over Raksha and Feldric, and
threatened to wash Tom from his
vantage point.

"Do something!" Kapra screeched.
"Stop that boy!"

"I can't," Feldric spluttered. "If
I use my magic, I'll hit Raksha."

Raskha tried to claw at Tom, but
he slid back through the hole left by

Sepron's tooth. One of the claws snagged at his ankle, drawing blood, but he ignored the pain. He saw Epos dive, snapping with her beak again. Raksha suddenly stumbled in the water.

That must be Sepron's doing! he thought. *She's snapping at his ankles.*

Tom went to work on the remaining tokens. With sweat pouring into his eyes, and arms that felt like molten lead, he managed to smash out Tagus's horse-shoe, and Nanook's golden bell. As they fell away, he wondered if he'd ever recover them from the depths of the lake. He felt a pang of guilt at destroying his shield too: four holes had been punched through its surface.

But I had no other choice, Tom thought.

Through one of the holes, he saw Tagus shaking the snakes from his powerful horse's legs and stamping at the grass. Then he heard screams and shouts. Nanook, her full strength returned, was clutching Kapra and Feldric in her hairy fists. Feldric was trying to level his staff to strike, but Epos swooped past, snatching it from his hand with her beak.

Tom's heart swelled to see his old friend back. The Flame Bird dropped the weapon into the hands of Elenna below.

"Let me go!" wailed Kapra.

"Better do as they say!" Tom shouted. *I'm winning!* he realised. And with only Elenna and the Avantians to help him.

With a growl, Nanook opened her

hands. The Gorgonian witch and
wizard plummeted into the lake,
screaming. After a few moments they
bobbed to the surface, drenched and
bedraggled, and dragged themselves
out of the water. Elenna pointed the

brass end of the staff towards them.

"One move, and you'll be a pile of burning clothes!" she said.

Silver bared his teeth and snarled, padding back and forth in front of the prisoners. Tagus reared on his hooves on the bank in front of the Beast, with Storm at his side. Sepron sent up wave after wave to blind the Mirror Demon.

"It's time to end this," Tom said, as he managed to prise out the last two tokens with the dagger. As each fell loose, he felt the tide turning in his favour. Arcta gave a defiant roar as he tore up a colossal tree. The Good Beast brandished it like a club, ready to attack.

The heat of flames on his face made Tom peer up. Silhouetted against the night sky, Ferno opened his jaws.

Fire blazed beneath his teeth, and his wings spread wide.

Tom was utterly exhausted but, at last, all the Beasts were free.

CHAPTER FIVE

CLASH OF THE BEASTS

Ferno dived towards the Lake of Light, skimming the surface and blasting flames. Raksha tried to grab at him as he swept past, but the Fire Dragon was too quick. The water boiled and hissed under the heat sent out from his body, and Tom made out Sepron sinking out of sight into the safety of the depths. The lake seemed to shrink, revealing more of the

muddy banks. When Ferno reached
the end of the stretch of water, he
turned and arced back for a second

pass, repeating his action.

He's shrinking the lake with his heat!
Tom realised. "Go, Ferno!"

Raksha howled and shuddered as
though racked with pain. Suddenly
Tom felt the armour press him tighter
against the Beast's chest. Almost as
though it was shrinking... Was the
Mirror Demon growing smaller and
less dangerous as the lake
disappeared?

I have to get out, before I'm crushed!
Tom thought.

Epos had joined Ferno, and sent
her fireballs spinning into the water.
Tom managed to scramble out from
the bottom of the armour, and swung
out onto the bank beside Storm. He
quickly jumped into the saddle and
looked back at Raksha. Yes, the Beast
had definitely shrunk. He was trying

to pull his hooves free of the sticky mud, bellowing in anger as the lake sizzled around him. The snakes around his head hung slack, and the scales on his legs seemed to have vanished. Tom rode around the edge of the water towards Elenna and Silver. When he glanced at the lake again, Raksha's shaggy fur had disappeared. He had slimy, brown skin like an eel.

"Fight back!" shouted Kapra, still at Elenna's mercy. Feldric knelt beside his mistress, his head in his hands.

"The Beast is losing his power!" Elenna told them. "There's nothing you can do about it."

Ferno and Epos kept up their barrage of fire, and the lake shrank further. Raksha stumbled out, armour flashing, and collapsed in the mud. As the Mirror Demon struggled to rise, Arcta strode angrily towards the Beast, great fists raised and ready to fight.

"Attack!" called Kapra, feebly. She seemed to be losing some of her power now that Raksha was almost defeated.

The Beast managed to summon a small fireball in his palm, but a wave of water from Sepron extinguished it. Arcta and the Mirror Demon stared at one another with their single eyes. Tom drew his sword, spurred Storm's flanks and galloped over. He turned in the saddle, to face the six Beasts, and buried his sword in its sheath.

"You can go home now and protect Avantia," he said gravely.

Tagus was first to lower his head, turn and walk away, then Sepron plunged back beneath the remaining water. Tom knew that whatever magic had brought her here was now taking her back to the Western

Ocean. Arcta's arms dropped to his sides, and Nanook's heaving chest stilled as calmness returned to her heart. Epos swooped past with a caw and then beat her powerful wings, climbing away. Last of all Ferno breathed a sigh of smoke and soared over the ridge of the valley, out of sight.

As Nanook, Arcta and Tagus bounded back towards their homes, Tom felt a surge of pride. After everything they'd been through, his victorious friends had proved themselves the rightful guardians of Avantia.

"No!" shouted Elenna.

Tom heard a squelch at his back, and twisted around. A fist smacked wetly into his stomach, lifting him out of Storm's saddle and throwing

him onto the bank. Raksha shoved
Storm into the shallows and lunged
after him. Tom rolled aside, winded,
as a hoof descended. He pushed
himself back up the bank. The Mirror
Demon now looked like a mass of
mud, his skin even slimier. His face
was featureless black ooze, apart
from a gaping, sucking mouth that
let out a deathly wail.

"Kill him!" Kapra ordered the Beast.

Tom found himself against a boulder, with nowhere else to run. He drew his sword, but Raksha knocked it from his hand. The blade sank into the mud, just out of reach. As the Beast's mouth descended towards his head, Tom felt sure he was about to die.

CHAPTER SIX

FRIEND OR FOE?

There was a flash of Storm's hooves, and Raksha's head jerked sideways. The Mirror Demon toppled over with a groan. Storm stood proudly before Tom, ready to protect his master.

"Thanks!" Tom gasped. As Raksha staggered upright again, Tom gripped Storm's dangling reins to heave himself up. He pulled his sword free of the mud, and brandished it at the Beast. Raksha let out a moan and

lumbered forward, but Tom slashed
with his sword. The trusty blade
sliced through the strap holding the
Beast's armour, and the pieces fell
from his body into the mud. Raksha
stood before him, utterly defenceless,
his body a slimy brown mass of clay.
He began to shrink further, his body
slipping into the mud at his feet. He
was disappearing before Tom's eyes.
Soon he was no taller than a man.

"No!" wailed Feldric.

"It's over," said Tom. He pointed his
sword towards the remains of the
lake, a pool just a few paces across.
"Go back to where you came from."

The Beast's shoulders sagged and
he turned his head towards Kapra
and Feldric.

"You coward!" screeched Kapra.
"Call yourself a Beast?"

"Why don't you fight your own
battles?" came another voice from
the top of the hill overlooking the

lake. Tom turned to see a small, squat figure creeping towards them. As a shaft of moonlight fell on her face, he saw it was Petra

"My daughter!" gasped Kapra. "My wonderful child! Come, help us! Show these Avantian children the meaning of pain."

"Don't help her, Petra!" shouted Tom. "You're better than her."

Petra lifted both hands in front of her face, and muttered a spell. Orange light fizzed between her palms. With a flick of her wrist, a sparking whip uncoiled from from her hand. Tom flinched, but instead of lashing him, the whip coiled around Raksha's middle. The Mirror Demon snarled and struggled weakly, but Petra gave the magical rope a tug.

"Come on!" Petra said. "Get back

where you belong!"

Kapra started forward, but the Avantians brandished their weapons in front of her.

What remained of the Mirror Demon stood at the water's edge. "Where's the mirror?" Petra asked. "We need it to help Raksha back to his home."

Feldric clutched his tunic. "You can't have it!"

Elenna whistled and Silver pounced upwards, placing his paws on the wizard's chest. Feldric fell down with a splat. The wolf leaned over his face, white fangs bared.

"All...right," Feldric managed. "Here it is." He reached inside his clothes and with a shaking hand withdrew the mirror. An Avantian woman snatched it out of his grasp.

"Reflect the moonlight at the water," said Tom. "Or what water's left," he muttered to himself. The lake was tiny now.

The farmer held the mirror up. Petra gave Raksha a shove into the last of the water, and the Beast sank out of sight. A few bubbles broke the surface, but as the moonlight struck the pool, the water became smooth. Then a small eddy appeared, deepening into a spiral. With a sucking sound, the water disappeared.

Tom took the mirror, and dropped it on the ground. He brought his heel down hard, shattering the glass and bending the frame out of shape. "Raksha won't be coming back," he said. "He deserves to be left in peace now."

"You traitor," Kapra shouted at Petra. "You're no daughter of mine!"

"I'd rather not be," Petra replied. "Shouldn't you be going home too?"

"I think that's a very good idea," muttered a voice.

Kerlo stood before the remains of the portal, his robes swirling around him. His lips curved into a small smile, and he beckoned Kapra and Feldric towards him with a crooked finger. "I suggest you say your farewells."

The blood drained from Feldric's

face, and Elenna trained an arrow on Kapra. "Move it!" she said.

Pursued by Silver and the armed Avantians, the witch and wizard shuffled towards the Gatekeeper.

"Are you sure you want them back in Gorgonia?" asked Tom.

Kerlo nodded. "They'll face justice in their own kingdom," he replied.

"Do you know anything of Taladon? He's been in Gorgonia with King Hugo and Aduro." Tom still couldn't understand why they had done nothing to help in this battle.

Kerlo smiled wisely. "Your father's Quests have taken him to the far reaches of our kingdom. I could have called on him, but then. Well..." He gave a small shrug. "Then I wouldn't have seen the hero Tom in action!"

Tom almost laughed with surprise. Kerlo had allowed him to face Raksha alone.

"I knew you could pull it off," the Gatekeeper said.

He stepped aside as Feldric entered the portal. Kapra, though, turned, and narrowed her eyes. She pointed a long nail at Tom. "You haven't heard the last of—"

Elenna shoved her through the portal before she could finish. "Good riddance!" she said.

"What about her?" asked Kerlo, nodding beyond them. Petra sat on the opposite bank, looking glum.

"Leave her," said Tom. "She's no threat for the moment."

"Very well," said the Gatekeeper. "I bid you farewell."

He backed away, and the portal swallowed him. The air closed up, concealing the red sky beyond. They'd laid eyes on Gorgonia for the last time.

CHAPTER SEVEN

ALL IN A DAY'S WORK

"I can see something in the mud!" said the Avantian farmer who'd given Tom the the magical dagger.

Tom tensed. Surely Raksha hadn't returned...

But it wasn't a Beast. In the centre of the mud, where the Lake of Light had once been, an object sparkled gold in the moonlight. Tom trudged towards it, his hope growing.

Kneeling down on the wet ground, his reached for the object, scraping off dirt. It was Nanook's golden bell. He wiped away more mud, and felt the wood of his shield. Breathing hard, he lifted it free and gasped.

His shield was intact, and all six tokens were safely embedded in the surface.

"I thought..." Elenna began.

"Me too!" said Tom, "but whatever magic gave it to Raksha has returned it to normal!"

He threaded his arm through the straps. "That feels better!"

"Wait until I tell the rest of the village about this!" said one of the Avantians, a teenage boy.

"You mustn't," said Tom, sternly. "We've saved the kingdom today – but others mustn't know of this. No one can know that the Beasts protect us."

The boy who'd spoken nodded solemnly. "I won't tell anyone."

"Me neither," said a woman.

One by one, the rest agreed.

"Return to your homes," Tom said. "And thank you all."

The farmers shook Tom and Elenna's hands, then set off to their villages. Tom shivered in the night air and stroked Storm's nose.

"We should head back too," said

Elenna, crouching beside Silver and ruffling her wolf's fur. "Aduro and Taladon are due back from their mission with King Hugo tomorrow."

"Should we say goodbye to her first?" asked Tom, gesturing towards Petra. She still sat alone further up the valleyside. Leading Storm by the reins, Tom approached her. Despite all their differences in the past, he felt a pang of sympathy for the young witch. "I want to thank you," he said. "It was a brave thing you did, standing up to your mother. I know we haven't always seen eye to eye—"

"Save your breath, Tom!" Petra snapped, eyes blazing behind a curtain of greasy hair. "I acted the way I did for *my* sake, not for yours." She scurried away to the crest of the hill, then turned back. "Don't go thinking we're friends," she said. "Next time our paths cross, it's business as usual."

As she disappeared from sight, Tom faced Elenna. His friend shrugged, and grinned. "Looks like a leopard doesn't change its spots."

They climbed into Storm's saddle, and rode out of the valley, with Silver running tirelessly alongside. At the edge of the Forest of Fear, Tom looked back. Perhaps it was because the moon had disappeared behind the clouds, but the valley below seemed cast in shadow. In fact, he wasn't really sure he could see it at all any more.

"I don't think we'll ever find it again," said Elenna.

"I'm not sure I want to," Tom replied.

By dawn they passed through Elderval again. Some people were getting ready for market, and others were rebuilding fences and walls knocked down by the Gorgonians. In the busy preparations for the new day, no one seemed to notice Tom and Elenna riding along the main street. *I prefer it that way*, Tom thought.

It was almost midday by the time they reached King Hugo's castle.

They stabled Storm, and washed the worst of the dirt from their faces and hands. The two children from earlier were playing in the courtyard. Tom gave them a wave as they climbed the steps to the banquet hall.

As they entered, he saw that all the mirrors had returned to normal. Daltec stood waiting for them beside

Aduro, Taladon and the King.

"You're alive!" Tom said.

"Of course I am!" said the young apprentice, with a smile. Tom didn't know how the magic had been reversed, but he didn't care. Elenna laughed softly beside him and reached out to ruffle the young wizard's hair.

Taladon grinned at his son.

"It seems the Gorgonia trip was a waste of time. False alarm. Aduro tells me there may have been a small problem here?" His brow wrinkled with curiosity.

Tom and Elenna shared a happy glance. "Nothing we couldn't handle," said Tom.

"I knew Avantia would be safe in your hands," said Aduro, his eyes twinkling. He slapped a hand on Taladon's shoulder. "You have a son to be proud of."

"Oh, I know," Tom's father said, staring hard into his eyes. "I've always known that."

As the five of them sat down to plates of cold chicken, Silver settled at Elenna's feet, looking up hopefully for scraps. Tom had battled a Beast, Storm was being groomed in the palace stables and Avantia was safe again.

Raksha's gone, he thought, licking the grease from his lips as he ate. He couldn't help the shudder that passed over him. To have seen his six good friends used for evil – it was worse than anything Tom had ever imagined. Elenna winked at him from across the table, lightening his mood. She always knew the best thing to do. Today, Tom could eat in the banqueting hall and know that no evil witches or wizards were going to burst from the mirrors. For now... But Tom knew he could never completely relax. Who knew what other Quests lay ahead of him?

JOIN TOM ON HIS NEXT
BEAST QUEST SOON!

Win an exclusive
Beast Quest T-shirt and goody bag!

In every Beast Quest book the Beast Quest logo is hidden
in one of the pictures. Find the logo in this book and
make a note of which page it appears on.
Send the page number in to us.
Each month we will draw one winner to receive
a Beast Quest T-shirt and goody bag.

Send your entry on a postcard listing
the title of this book and the winning
page number to:

THE BEAST QUEST COMPETITION:
RAKSHA THE MIRROR DEMON
Orchard Books
338 Euston Road, London NW1 3BH
Australian readers should email:
childrens.books@hachette.com.au

New Zealand readers should write to:
Beast Quest Competition
4 Whetu Place, Mairangi Bay, Auckland, NZ
or email: childrensbooks@hachette.co.nz

Only one entry per child.
Final draw: OCTOBER 2012

You can also enter this competition
via the Beast Quest website: www.beastquest.co.uk

Join the Quest,
Join the Tribe

www.beastquest.co.uk

Have you checked out the Beast Quest website? It's the place to go for games, downloads, activities, sneak previews and lots of fun!

You can read all about your favourite beasts, download free screensavers and desktop wallpapers for your computer, and even challenge your friends to a Beast Tournament.

Sign up to the newsletter at www.beastquest.co.uk to receive exclusive extra content and the opportunity to enter special members-only competitions. We'll send you up-to-date info on all the Beast Quest books, including the next exciting series which features six brand-new Beasts!

Get 30% off all Beast Quest Books at www.beastquest.co.uk
Enter the code BEAST at the checkout.

All books priced at £4.99,
special bumper editions
priced at £5.99.

Orchard Books are available from all good bookshops, or can
be ordered from our website: www.orchardbooks.co.uk,
or telephone 01235 827702, or fax 01235 8227703.

Series 9: THE WARLOCK'S STAFF
COLLECT THEM ALL!

Malvel is up to his evil tricks again! The fate of all the lands is in Tom's hands...

978 1 40831 316 9

978 1 40831 317 6

978 1 40831 318 3

978 1 40831 319 0

978 1 40831 320 6

978 1 40831 321 3